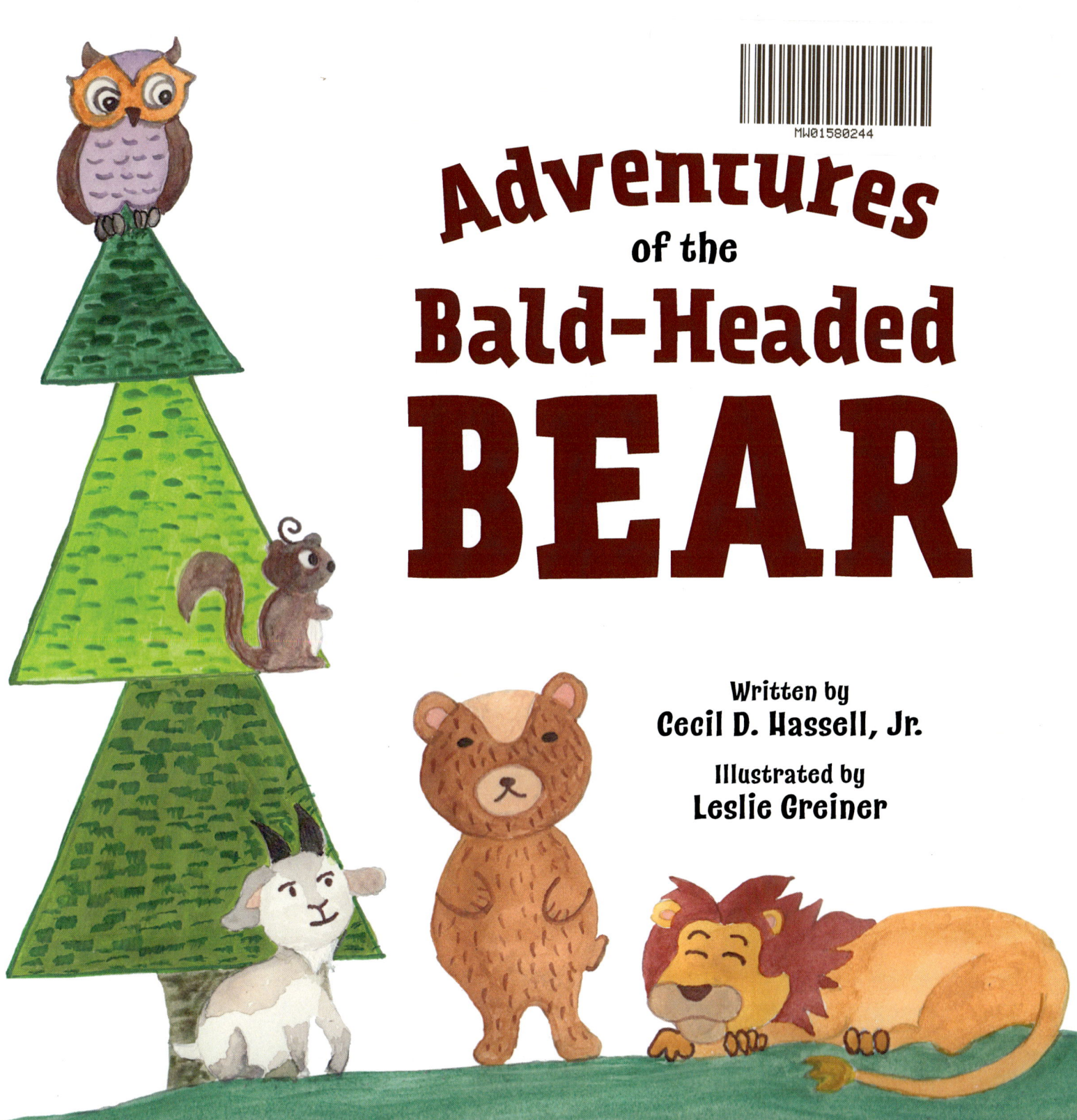

Copyright © 2023 by Cecil D. Hassell, Jr.

All rights reserved. No part of this book may
be used or reproduced by any means,
graphic, electronic or mechanical, including photocopying,
recording, taping or by any information storage retrieval
system, without the written permission of the author,
except in the case of brief quotations embodied in reviews.

Paperback ISBN 978-1-960007-32-2
eBOOK ISBN 978-1-960007-33-9

Published by
Little Blessing Books
an imprint of
Orison Publishers, Inc.
PO Box 188, Grantham, PA 17027
www.OrisonPublishers.com

Once upon a time,
There was a bald-headed bear,
Born to his parents
With not a bit of hair
On the top of his head.

So he decided to search
For someone who knew
Where
He could find his hair.

"Oh, my beautiful bear,"
His mother said,
"You've no need to search
For hair
For your head.
You are perfectly fine without it.

"You are whole
And complete,
Very smart
And very neat,
Without a bit of hair
On your head."

As he walked among the trees
He encountered a squirrel,
With big, engaging eyes
And the cutest little curl
On the top of her head.

"Hello, little squirrel,"
The bald bear said.
"I love the little curl
On the top of your head."

"Oh you're so nice, so nice,"
Said the little squirrel,
Not once but twice.
And that made the bald bear smile.

He said, "I'm looking for hair
For the top of my head."
And that made the squirrel ask,
"Why?"

"Because all the other bears
Have hair on their heads."

"Oh," was her response,
But she only said it once.
Then she bounded
From the ground
To the top of his crown.

She curled into a circle,
Saying, "This should do.
I like me for your hair.
How about you?"

"No," said the bear.
"Thank you just the same."
But he did laugh
As he lumbered away.

After days and days,
He encountered a lion—
A very sad cat,
Who was just sitting there cryin'.

Why are you cryin'?"
The bear asked...
And then he saw
A great big thorn
In the lion's paw.

The bear
Bent down,
Placing a hand
On the lion's crown,
And he gently removed the thorn.

"Well..." said the bear,
"I've been looking for some hair."

The lion pondered, then he said,
"Let's see how my mane
Looks on your head!"

They arranged the mane
And then checked their reflection
In a puddle of rain.
"It looks silly," the bear said,
Shaking his head.
"Indeed," said the lion. "Quite inane!"

They both laughed.

"I can't help you," said the lion.
But I can give you this note
Written by a goat.

"She said if I was I ever in need,
To give her a call.
But thanks to your kind deed,
My injured paw
Feels AMAZING!"

The bear was off,
Clutching the note,
And finally, he came
Upon the goat.

"What do you have there?"
Asked the goat of the bear.
"It looks like a note I gave to a lion."

"That's right!" said the bear.
"I found him cryin'
Because of a thorn
That was stuck in his paw—
Biggest thorn I ever saw!

"And I removed it."

"Ok," said the goat.
"How can I help you?"

"Well," said the bear,
Touching the top of his head,
"I'm in search of the hair
That should be up there."

The goat looked up,
Then she looked down
And saw some moss
Lying on the ground.
With a little toss,
It was on the bear's head.

"Now, that looks pretty cool…"
The nanny goat said.
Then they smiled at each other,
Shaking their heads.

"I can't help with hair,
But I do declare
That the wise, old owl
Might lend a hand."
The bear was ecstatic.
"That would be grand!"

Until he heard a hoot,
Or was it a howl?
He couldn't tell.
But he saw the owl.

And he told the owl
About the squirrel
With the curl,
The lion
Who was cryin',
And the goat
With the note,
And how he was determined
To find his hair.

The wise, old owl nodded
As he listened to the tale.
Then he plodded
To the bear
And leaned close.
"What did your mother say?"

As if reading his mind,
The owl was kind.
"You don't really need hair,"
He said, "there,
On the top of your head."

"Well, I guess not,"
Said the bear.
"I am a bald-headed bear, whole and complete."

"T'is true.
Hair or no hair,
A bear
You shall always be.
Don't you see?
Just be happy to be you,
Like I am glad to be me."

"Thank you!" said the bear,
Now happy to head home.
"It is nice to feel the air
On my hairless dome!"